A Rainbow at Night

The World in Words and Pictures by Navajo Children

chronicle books

SAN FRANCISCO

Book design by Learning Arts, Santa Fe, New Mexico
Typeset in Weiss with Galahad Display
Printed in China

Library of Congress Information Available
ISBN: 0–8118–1294–4

Distributed in Canada by Raincoast Books
8680 Cambie Street
Vancouver, B.C. V6P 6M9

Distributed in Australia and New Zealand
by CIS Cardigan Street
245–249 Cardigan Street, Carlton 3053 Australia

10 9 8 7 6 5 4 3 2 1

Chronicle Books
275 Fifth Street
San Francisco, CA 94103

IN MEMORIUM

Steward Sam   1974–1992
Jheri Billie   1975–1994

Two bright colors of the rainbow
Two spirits who now look upon us
offering their blessings from another place

This book is dedicated to the creative spirit in all children.

INTRODUCTION

Ya'at'eeh. Welcome to the beautiful and imaginative world of Navajo children. *A Rainbow at Night* was created so that a special group of Navajo children could share with you their art, ideas about making art, and introduce you to their vibrant culture. The term culture means the ideas, traditions, and arts of a certain group of people living in a particular landscape or period of time. This book is guided by the idea that if we all learn a little bit about each other's culture and ways of living, and treat each other with respect, then the world can be a better place.

Navajos often tell about themselves through story. The story of this book begins with a child's question. Ten-year old Jheri Billie asked me "Have you ever seen a rainbow at night?" As her art teacher and friend, I did not immediately know what to say. Having lived in the community of Montezuma Creek, Utah and worked with the children for eight years I felt I had seen and learned a great deal, but this was different. I thought she had a rainbow confused with the halo that forms around the moon when nights are cold.

"Well, have you?" she persisted, a smile growing on her face.

I replied that I hadn't and wondered what sort of joke this would turn out to be. But this was no joke. Jheri went on to describe in great detail just where and when she had seen the rainbow at night. And when I questioned her she emphatically replied, "Yes! It was a rainbow! It had all the colors!"

Rainbows and their colors are important to the Navajos. When they appear it means that the spirits who guard over them are present. When you see a rainbow after a summer rain they say it's a blessing from the spirits

because water in the desert means life. Rainbows are a favorite for children to draw. They make rainbows over hogans, bicycles, trucks and ninjas. We can all see daytime rainbows but, have you ever seen a rainbow at night? Jheri's question asks us to take a closer look at the world around us, to see and express ourselves in a way others do not. To see a rainbow at night you must also understand where the Navajo come from, how they live, and what they think. In this way, you can begin to see through the children's eyes.

These young Navajo artists, ages 6–13, live in the communities of Montezuma Creek, Bluff, Mexican Hat, Monument Valley and Navajo Mountain on the Utah portion of the Navajo Nation. The Navajo refer to themselves as *Diné*, The People. They traditionally live within the Four Corners area of the United States where Arizona, New Mexico, Colorado and Utah come together. Navajoland is a mixture of broad sandy valleys and steep sandstone-capped mesas and buttes. From the high points of the land the children can see the four sacred mountains that encircle their world. Other mountains, deep canyons, rivers and lakes can also be found. There is snow and rain, burning sun, wind and frost. There are also eagles and hawks, ravens, rabbits, deer and the troublesome Coyote, a character found in many Navajo stories. Navajo children spend a lot of time outside with nature and have a special relationship with the earth. Their parents and grandparents tell them that the earth is their mother and that she is clothed with plants and animals who give them food, medicine and knowledge. Because of this strong connection to the land, today's Navajo child sees the world differently. They not only see the trees and rocks upon it but the spirit that dwells inside. It is the same for all of creation—plants, animals, mountains and rivers. The Navajo see that everything in the world is alive!

In making the art, I asked the children to think about themselves and to paint or draw from their personal experience. While many children still participate in traditional ceremonies and daily chores, the balance of their lives include the same things as other children—television and movies, school and homework, peer pressure and self-esteem, laughter and anger, friendships, riding bikes, teasing, running, pizza, and the process of growing up. The art in this book is a blend of traditional Navajo ways of living and modern ideas.

To make the art, the children learned the skills that all artists know. They learned to make all the colors of their own rainbows by mixing yellow, red, blue, black and white. They learned to make a pencil talk by practicing sketching, shading and shadow. Watercolor, tempera, oil pastel, and marker techniques were used. Most importantly, the children learned to apply their art knowledge to the creation of their own image and to think about the process of art as a conversation between the artist, materials and idea.

"In these paintings you'll find many symbols, designs and ideas that you may not understand," says twelve-year old Delphine Tanner, "but if you look closely, read our comments, and just think about it, you might understand."

Through their work, Navajo children have made a portion of their world visible to you. You are invited to enter this world and take a look.

—Bruce Hucko,
Children's "Art Coach"

STEPHANIE
MANYBEADS
AGE 11

The Navajo believe that every part of nature is related to them like family. To the Navajo the land is alive. Across the Navajo Nation traditional people rise early, face the east and say, "Good Morning Father Sun." Navajos greet a wise old tree or animal of knowledge like horned toad with respect by saying, *Ya'at'eeh Shichei,* meaning "Hello Grandfather." Other animals and plants are called cousin, brother, or sister. Stephanie sees the early morning sun as a friend and painted her using watercolor on wet paper.

"Her name is Sunrise girl.
She is fresh.
Her vivid colors are shining her reflection on the ocean
in the morning.
Her hair is like an orange in the sun,
red as a cherry squished.
Her face is yellow as lemon that has sat in the hottest sun
for a week
Her reflection is vivid.
The ocean is blue as blueberries.
She awakes to light the day."

What is your relationship to Nature? Think of the sun, the moon or a particular mountain or river. Choose an element of nature that you want to bring into your family. Paint or draw it so it fills the paper. How will you greet it?

SUNRISE GIRL

watercolor

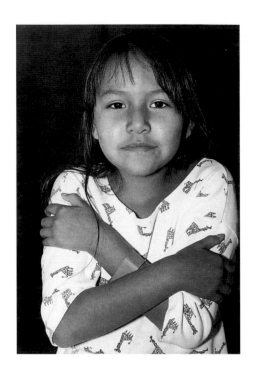

CATHLENA PLUMMER
AGE 8

Navajo culture and history is passed to future generations through story. Stories teach the Navajo how they came to be and how to live. Stories are traditionally told by an elder in the winter around a warm fire.

Many stories, like the story of "Water Ox," describe how the world was created. Traditionally called Water Monster, he is said to have the fine fur of an otter and horns like a buffalo. Water Monster controls mountain springs and rivers and is known to be everybody's friend. He is visited when there is a drought. Cathlena used watercolor and simple large figures to create her own picture to match the story.

" The men are telling Water Ox that they want water in their land. Water Ox makes it rain and makes trees grow. He changes color. Water Ox is mad because the men interrupt him. He changed to a dark color. And then Water Ox told them that he could make it rain. "

What is your family's story? Where did you come from? Ask your parents and grandparents, and listen. Draw the most important parts of the story large on your paper. Add details to clothing and other objects. Write or tell the story of the picture to another family member.

R A I N B O W   M E N   M E E T   W A T E R   O X

pencil and watercolor

The Navajo live in the desert. Many people think of this land as dry and dull. But it is not. Earl is used to seeing a variety of colors ranging from bright orange cliffs to the deep purple of shadows. Navajoland can also be very green with many brightly colored flowers covering the ground. The desert sky is often clear blue. At other times, it is blessed with rain clouds that can be gray, pink or deep orange. Navajo country is not one color. Earl chose a blend of blue and purple paint to make rain and wiggled his brush around on wet paper to get his favorite kind of sky just right. He then created his own land by using thick paint.

" It's a pretend place. There's a house, a rock, a man and a highway. There are road and rug designs covering the picture. I used watercolor and colored pens. When I look at it I think the man came out of his house and he was happy! **"**

Imagine a landscape all your own. The sky, the land and everything on it is created by you. What would the sky look like? What color would it be? What kinds of rocks do you like? Do you prefer mountains, mesas, canyons, hills or a beach? Like Earl, add a second layer to your art by drawing a design or pattern over the land. Look around for ideas. What is it about your special place that makes you happy?

A PRETEND PLACE

watercolor, oil pastel, marker

MAX BENALLY
AGE 10

NAVAJO
SCARECROW
colored pencil, watercolor

Home to the Navajo is a place not an address. The land is most important to them. When asked, "Where do you live?" most Navajo children will answer with directions that refer to the landscape. "Across the canyon." "Over by Red Mesa." "By that rock with the face on it." Their backyards stretch out for miles and the children know every canyon and hillside in it. A "next door neighbor" may live up to five miles away! Since there are few fences, land is often divided by use of landmarks or pillars of stone. Some of these pillars are also shrines. While roaming the land with friends, Max walked up a sandstone hill and found this tall pile of rocks. He emphasized the pillar by drawing it large and giving each rock its own color.

These rocks are at Red Mesa, at the Topaha's. The rocks are all different colors. The pile of rocks keeps Coyote away from the sheep.

What marks the boundary of "your backyard." Look on your own land and find an important object that marks a side or corner of your property. It could be a tree, a rock, a garden, a wall or fence. Draw it. Add lines to show texture and what is in the background. What colors do you see? What unique sounds do you hear? What would you do in a backyard that stretches out for miles?

SHAWN BLACK
AGE 9

BEAUTIFUL
DAY AT MY
HOUSE
colored pencil

" I live in this trailer with my mom and dad. I made it with colored pencils. Where I live there's a mesa behind my house. It looks beautiful. My grandpa lives in the hogan. I help him chase the sheep in and he helps me find some lost sheep. **"**

What makes a beautiful day at your own house? Is it the weather, a special activity or the landscape around your house? Is it having grandparents or someone special nearby? While spending time at home listen for that feeling that says, "This is a great day to be home." Draw whatever gives you that feeling. What colors and sounds represent that beautiful feeling?

A hogan is the traditional house of the Navajos. There are two kinds of hogans, male and female. Both are traditionally made from earth and pine logs. The male hogan has a steep roof. The female hogan is round and it is the only kind lived in by families. The door of a hogan always opens to the east to greet Father Sun. Although many Navajo children today live in square roomed homes and trailers with water and electricity, there is almost always a hogan somewhere on family land. Shawn carefully drew the mesa, hogan, house, and the people in them with colored pencils to make a beautiful day.

11

Many Navajo families depend upon sheep and goats to make a living. Their meat provides food. Their wool is woven into rugs or sold to buy things for the family. Generally owned by the women, sheep herds may range from a few dozen to over one hundred animals. Taking care of them is a family project. Beginning at about 5 years of age, children are taught to help care for the sheep. At school Tonya learned to paint with value, the lightness or darkness of a color, by adding white or black to her paint. After getting off the school bus she and her sister Earlene look for the family's sheep to herd them home.

" The girl is chasing the sheep in. It is my sister Earlene. She has 20 sheep. This picture is by my house. The sun is going down between 2 mesas. They look like rugs. **"**

How do you help with your family's work? Draw yourself, a brother, sister or parent performing a family chore. Make the people large and important. Like Tonya you can divide the background into a line pattern using straight, diagonal or curved lines and color each section of your picture with different values.

E A R L E N E ' S   J O B

tempera

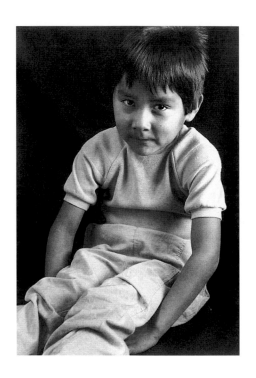

In a traditional Navajo family, wealth is measured by the amount of livestock they own. Horses, cows, sheep, and goats once were (and are still often) used instead of money. Horses are important and are mainly kept to help with the sheep. Even young girls and boys like Artimio help care for the horses. Many children learn to ride well before they become teenagers. Some grow up to ride in rodeos as Navajo cowboys and cowgirls.

" J.R. and Sarah are my horses. Sarah is blue. They are just standing. The horses are eating hay. The hay is black. **"**

ARTIMIO HASCON
AGE 5

What pets do you have? Watch them to see where their personality shows through. It may be how they move or a look on their face. Or, like Artimio, you can use color and many small strokes to help show your pet's personality.

J . R . AND SARAH

oil pastel

KATHERINE TONEY
AGE 11

Wild animals are a natural part of the Navajo world. Navajos believe that people and animals once lived and talked together. Today animals live separately but are still revered. Bear, Deer, Snake, Coyote and many other animals play important roles in traditional ceremonies and stories. Eagle is sacred. He carries the people's prayers to Father Sky. It is an honor to wear or be given an eagle feather. Katherine wears one of Eagle's feathers in her hair when she dances at Indian celebrations called pow-wows.

"When my dad was driving around he saw a bird, an eagle, with different colors on it—for real!—and it was kind of bald and had some blood on it's cheek. That's where I got the idea from, when my dad told me. The colors came from my head so it would look pretty. You probably can't see the third bird because it is made with the other two birds and the sky. I put names on the small birds, the initials of my friends. The colors are this way to put excitement in the bird."

What's your favorite wild animal? Katherine drew her birds from the perspective of being in the sky flying alongside them. Draw your animal from a different angle. Put "excitement" in your work by using the patterns, colors, and dress of what you and your friends wear.

16

T H R E E   P U N K   B I R D S

liquitex

Navajos share the land with wild creatures, often finding them in their backyards. According to Navajo tradition, many of these animals have individual powers. Snakes have power over water and rain. Because water is so important to human life, snakes, especially rattlesnakes, are to be taken seriously. Calvert placed two strong designs on top of each other to make a powerful picture of a powerful creature.

**CALVERT NORTON
AGE 11**

"I came out one day and looked down through the porch. It is made out of metal and has diamond holes in it. I saw this. I guess my dog picked it up and brought it home. It looks like a brain. The snake is the cerebral cortex. The background is the top part of the skull. Snakes scare some people.**"**

What wild animals live in your backyard? If it had a special power in nature what would that be? Draw that animal and pattern it with a design you find around your home. Write a story about that animal and how it uses its power.

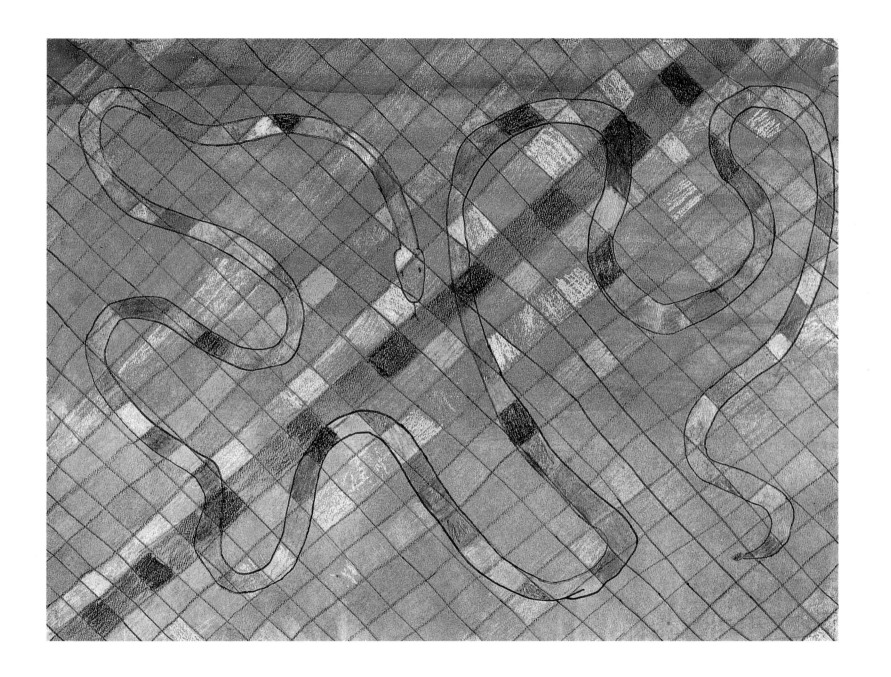

SNEAKY SNAKE

oil pastel, ink

ANGELA ATENE
AGE 11

Coyote stories are told throughout the Navajo Nation. Coyote, a trickster, acts like a human, trying to outsmart other animals in order to get something for himself. Because he is greedy and impatient his plans usually backfire. Once, while First Man was carefully placing stars in the sky in the patterns we know as constellations, Coyote came around. Thinking he could perform the task better and faster, he grabbed the remaining stars and threw them into the sky. That's why some areas of the sky are blank and other places, like the Milky Way, have many stars. If it were not for Coyote's haste the whole sky would be filled with star patterns. On cold winter evenings Angela and other Navajo children are entertained by Coyote stories. Through Coyote's actions, the Navajo teach their children about patience and being a good person.

" Coyote acts stupid. He stares at people, eats human being's food. He's trying to think the whole world. **"**

Do you know a Coyote or someone who is always making life difficult for others? A merry prankster? In some cultures, he is seen as Raven or Ananzi, the Spider. What does your trickster look like and what happens when he tries to fool others? Draw and color your figure using bold colors. Over and around your trickster show what trouble your trickster gets into!

COYOTE THINKING

markers and chalk

TOBY TOPAHA
AGE 13

Navajos try to maintain balance in all things. Many daily and ceremonial activities are concerned with maintaining good relationships with people and nature. The elders say that a good life is lived by balancing the needs of self, your people, nature and the spirits. The artistic idea of balance is seen in Navajo sandpaintings, weaving, and jewelry. Toby knows that balance is also important in painting and drawing. Balance is at work when all the images in a picture work well with each other.

"We were working with primary colors. First I sketched it out. It just popped up. The things shown are sandpainting, squaw dance, etc. The one where the lady is weaving is my grandma cause I see her like that a lot. Another lady is weaving a basket in the corner. In the corner is the land, how I see it when it's raining. The figure is a Rainbow "Yeibi-chei." The whole painting is what my grandparents do."

What are the activities that define and describe your family or culture? Using pencil begin to sketch them on paper. Make them work together. Is there a place for the land? How do the images you drew help keep your life in balance?

WHAT SOME NAVAJOS DO
watercolor

HARMAN RENTZ
AGE 6

YEI - BI - CHEI
markers

The Navajo believe that there are spirits who watch over them. *Yei-bi-chei* (yay-bi-chay) are the grandfather spirits. They are the most respected. They attend ceremonies, bless the land with rain, and act as guardians. They travel on rainbows and may appear and be watching from anywhere. They are much like people yet have supernatural powers. They can be generous, but may also get angry. They also have a sense of humor. Here are two different and personal visions of them.

" He's walking to his hogan. He will cook meat. He walks down the street from his grandma's. He was just sitting there. Sometimes he dances for sick people. He wears different colors. He likes feathers. A rainbow is touching him. He likes Rainbow 'cause it's raining. The plants grow. He touches the plant. It grows big. **"**

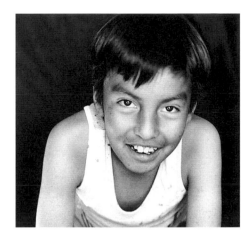

TYRONE THOMAS
AGE 10

YEI - BI - CHEI
WORKOUT
tempera

" I was thinking of olden days when I first made it up. It's funny to put old and new things together. I put things together that usually don't go together. Yei-bi-cheis don't work out. All I see is them dancing. They had to learn to dance somehow so I put them in a workout. **"**

What do you think your "spirit" or "creator" looks like? Does he or she act like a person? Where would you find the "spirit?" Draw your "spirit" in a human situation that mixes old and new images.

25

DARREN ETSITTY
AGE 12

A strong feeling of spirit is found in all Navajo beliefs. Prayers are made to the spirits of the dawn and sacred mountains. Spirits control the weather and are found in all parts of nature. Navajo people ask the spirits for assistance through ceremony. Traditional ceremonies are held in a hogan or outdoors at different times of the day. Today, ceremonies are also held in homes and teepees. The use of teepees is borrowed from Plains Indians by Navajo members of the Native American Church. Members of this church use the peyote cactus in a ceremony or "meeting" held during one night. Just like in many other churches the members pray and sing together, asking the "spirits" for blessings. While in this ceremony, Darren would have been praying for his own people and for you, too.

"This painting is in the morning. Everybody has been singing from the evening to morning for a person who is sick. The red and blue blankets are to protect the people in the teepee from chiindis, witchcraft, and all that stuff. After the meeting they'll eat. They have meetings whenever people get sick. I go sometimes. When I'm tired I don't go. I go to sleep."

Notice the smooth way the colors of morning light move across the teepee. Darren blended the edges of all his colors to make this stunning watercolor. What is your most powerful time of the day? What colors are in the sky, the land and the buildings around you then? Make a painting of your home or some other familiar scene blending the colors of your special time of day.

PEYOTE CHURCH

watercolor

MELISSA CLEVELAND
AGE 8

A medicine man is responsible for the spiritual well-being and health of the Navajo people. This includes asking the spirits for their blessings such as rain, good crops and abundant livestock. The health of the land is directly related to the health of the people. When one becomes "sick" both are understood to be "out of balance." A medicine man then conducts a ceremony to bring both back to good health. Today, traditional Navajo beliefs about spirit and health are sometimes divided. Many Navajo people visit clinics when they are sick, attend a Christian church to pray, and watch nature go its own way. Although the blending of cultures usually works well, Melissa shows what can happen when the connection between people and nature is broken—chaos!

❝The Indians are going to America and they went to go to Red Mesa Church—God! They are coming out of the church. When they came out of the church they were cold and it was raining with snow, and snowflakes were coming down. Their horns are so weird, one is crooked. They did not know how to sing like a medicine man.❞

Create a painting that you feel is spiritual. It may be your church or temple. Maybe it is a special place in nature where you go to think. The word "spirit" means different things to different people. What does it mean to you?

NAVAJO INDIANS

tempera

Navajo people recognize that there must be a balance of good and evil in the world. Stories of witchcraft are common in Navajoland. Evil spirits exist. No one really knows exactly what they look like or how they work. It takes the strong power of a medicine man to correct their evil deeds. Steward combined cultural images, the head of a coyote with the body of a Saturday morning cartoon super-hero, to create his vision of a Navajo *chiindi*.

❝*Chiindi* is someone in my dreams. In English he's like the devil. He does witchcraft, curses people and hypnotizes with his eyes. He disguises himself as a *maii* (coyote). The skull helps him do witchcraft. It's a human Anasazi head. The battle axe is to defend himself from other people. I see him late at night in my dreams. I sit back and watch to see what he does.**❞**

Many cultures have something frightening in them. The devil, the bogeyman, or zombies. What creatures give you the creeps? What power do they have over you? Draw them by combining different kinds of pictures you've seen and perhaps you can get power over them.

MY CHIINDI

colored pencil

AVELINA REED
AGE 11

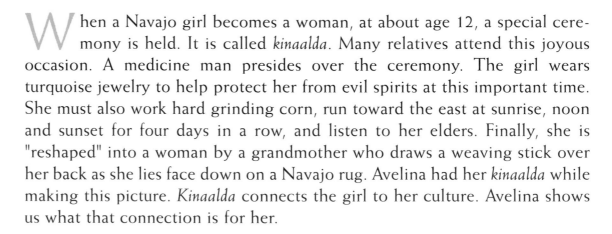

When a Navajo girl becomes a woman, at about age 12, a special ceremony is held. It is called *kinaalda*. Many relatives attend this joyous occasion. A medicine man presides over the ceremony. The girl wears turquoise jewelry to help protect her from evil spirits at this important time. She must also work hard grinding corn, run toward the east at sunrise, noon and sunset for four days in a row, and listen to her elders. Finally, she is "reshaped" into a woman by a grandmother who draws a weaving stick over her back as she lies face down on a Navajo rug. Avelina had her *kinaalda* while making this picture. *Kinaalda* connects the girl to her culture. Avelina shows us what that connection is for her.

❝ I like the colors of sunset. I like to draw mountains. I like to wear jewelry so I drew it. My father made them. The brown object is the grinding stone that my grandma uses daily to grind the yellow corn. I have a vase like this at home. We put sagebrush in there, and flowers. I chose these things to protect me. **❞**

Avelina chose and arranged objects that are special to her into a still life composition. Gather together those objects you feel are special to you (or that protect you). Arrange them as you like. Draw and color them.

S U N S E T   C U L T U R E

watercolor, colored pencil

TRISTA THOMAS
AGE 8

34

Navajo dances usually take place during a healing ceremony. They are traditionally held outdoors in a remote area, but nowadays are often found in school gymnasiums. Some dances are strictly ceremonial while others are social. Some are both. Trista's Round Dance is part of a summer ceremony held outside. Several hundred people may attend the ceremony and participate in the dance. Trista's image shows an outhouse because there are no modern facilities where the dance is. If you look closely you can see Trista's attention to detail and humor at work.

" I was going to play at the field. I was going to play with my friends but they would not play with me. When I was walking back I saw a pow-wow in the gym. I went to my house to change into my traditional clothes. When I got to the dance I saw feathers on the men sticking out like a turkey on their backs. They have bells that jingle. I started to dance. The men were singing, the drum was pounding. I danced in the round dance with the people. When they round dance they skip and they hold hands. **"**

Dance can be fun to paint because the bodies can be full of action and color. What dances do you know? Draw several large figures dancing and pay attention to the angles the arms and legs make. Which way are they facing? Add the surrounding environment. Can you find a place to hide something funny in your picture?

THE ROUND DANCE

tempera

VALERIE PHILLIPS
AGE 11

RAINBOW RUG
oil pastel

Rug weaving is one of the most widely known Navajo art forms. It demands a lot of skill and patience. Weaving is a long process of shearing the sheep, cleaning and preparing the wool, dyeing and spinning the wool, and finally setting the loom up to weave. Many girls learn to weave when they are young, but Valerie didn't. Instead, she put the strong design found in traditional rugs into a drawing. Looking around the art room, Valerie found an idea for color and combined it with a Navajo rug pattern, blending two different ideas to make a new one.

I was looking around in the art studio and I saw a picture of an Indian by John Nieto. I got the idea from inside of the face. Then, instead of drawing an Indian I drew a rug A RUG! I drew a blue rectangle and then I colored it in. There. It's called Rainbow Rug because of the colors.

Navajo rugs have wonderful geometric designs. What can you find around you that also has strong patterns and design? Use it as an inspiration to create your own rug design. Draw the outline and fill in the pattern. Give it a fun title!

VANESSA NAKAI
AGE 11

WEIRD RUG
colored pencil,
oil pastel

Many Navajo children have artists in their family. Vanessa lives with her grandmother, a skilled weaver. When she comes home from school Vanessa has many choices. To help with chores or do homework? To learn rug weaving from her grandmother or watch TV? The demands and distractions of modern life require children and adults to make difficult choices. In Weird Rug, Vanessa makes a strong statement about the dilemma of keeping traditional art forms alive.

" The design on the rug came from my head. My art teacher helped me with the idea, but I put it together the way I wanted it. All the time I spend watching TV I could be weaving a rug. "

Television has had a great impact on everyone's life. Often helpful, it can also trap us and keep us from performing other activities. How has TV affected your life? Make a drawing that shows this.

37

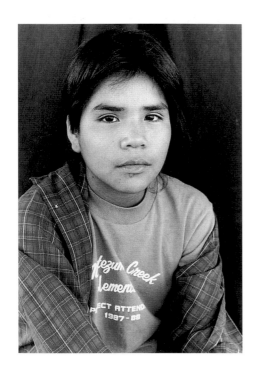

EUGENIA CAPITAN
AGE 11

Navajo is a visual language where it is more important to describe the shape and action of something than to know its name. A truck, a football, a horse, and a mountain have their own shape. Like many good artists Eugenia knows that good ideas can come from the world around her. She overlapped the shapes and outlined them in color to create a painting of objects that had pleasing shapes.

"All of the ideas came from my mind, except the eagle. It came from a picture, but I didn't draw the whole body. The piano, vase, and teepee are things I like. The piano sounds out. The lines are the music the piano makes. The purple vase is a Navajo shape. I used the teepee because I like it. We use our teepee for peyote meetings or a Navajo ceremony when grandma is sick or when it's somebody's birthday. I used a toothbrush to make the dots. When I look at the eagle and other things I see wonderful shapes."

Think about the wonderful shapes around you. Some may be natural and others made by humans. Draw or paint some of them on large paper overlapping some. Outline all with other colors. To get the dots, dip a toothbrush in paint, turn it toward the paper and run your finger over the bristles to release the paint. Watch your aim!

WONDERFUL SHAPES

tempera

ROLLAND D. LEE
AGE 12

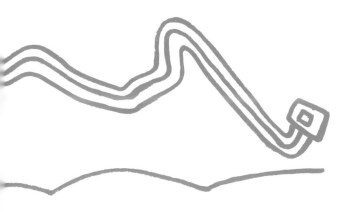

There is no word for art in the Navajo language. The creation of beauty is seen as a natural part of being human. Movement is also a natural and important part of the language. There are more verbs than nouns in the language. Navajo people are always doing something. Herding sheep, chopping wood, fixing cars and cooking are common activities. Though they may have "jobs" like teaching school and managing an oil field, many family members create beauty through drawing, beading, weaving, carving, painting and pottery. Rolland looks to the activities of his family for inspiration.

" I always paint the sky and background first. Then the mountain and the sand dune. There's a sand dune like this at my grandma's house and I can see Sleeping Ute Mountain. The mountain looked plain sitting there so I made the sun rays coming from it. I drew different things in each space between the rays. I made the dark plants and their shadows, not like it really is, to make it more interesting. All the ideas come from both sides of my family, the things they do.

When I started I didn't have the faintest idea of what it was going to look like. I draw one thing at a time which leads me to the next space. When I start to draw more ideas come to me. At first it doesn't connect, but the more I look and work on it, it does! **"**

Think of the many things that the different members of your family do. What objects represent your parents, brothers, sisters, grandparents, cousins, aunts and uncles, and yourself? Start drawing them. Fit them together like a puzzle. Like Rolland follow your brain as it suggests ideas to you. When an idea comes, use it and as you draw listen to yourself for other ideas until the paper is filled.

C U L T U R A L   M O U N T A I N

watercolor, colored pencil

The goal of Navajo life is to live in harmony with all of creation. In many Navajo songs and prayers you hear the word *hozho*. This word roughly translates as a combination of good health, happiness, order, balance and beauty. Repeated at the end of a song or prayer it reminds all people to live in beauty. As a final art assignment Elisa was asked to use her newly learned painting skills to create something about being Navajo. Instead of making a picture of hogans and sheep she chose to show us her vision of *hozho*.

**ELISA BLACKGOAT
AGE 12**

" The idea started with a postcard of one bird with a rainbow in its beak. I wanted to have something Navajo in there so I decided to make them all sing together. I added hills and mountains because I like them. "

What is your vision of how our world can live in balance, happiness, and beauty? Decide on what is most important to you to achieve well-being. Create a piece of art where your thoughts and concerns all sing together. May your art, like your life, be lived in beauty.

T H E   S I N G I N G   B I R D S

watercolor, liquitex

"Rainbow at Night"
artists not featured in
this book are:

Paul Atcitty

Adrienne Begay

Janella Benally

Janice Benally

Cerelia Dee

Lavena Freeman

Tyson Hopkins

Lyle Jones

Vandever Merritt

Ivan Miles

Cherolyn Mustache

Chavez Nakai

Tyrone Nakai

Lyle R. Phillips

Rodi Reed

Tonya Silas

Calbert Thomas

Howard Todachinnie

Josephene Warren

ACKNOWLEDGMENTS

It is customary when introducing oneself in Navajo to offer your clan (family) names on both the mother's and father's side. These terms of relatedness help your audience establish their connection to you and emphasize the importance of the individual to the group. It establishes family. The family associated with this work begins with the forty-two "Rainbow at Night" artists, their families, friends and communities; and the hundreds of children who attended art classes. Without their friendship, generous spirits, good humor and persistence there would be no rainbows in my life at all!

While living in Montezuma Creek I befriended the families of many children. I thank the following families for making me feel at home: the Joe's, Sam's, Billie's, Nakai's and Topaha's of Montezuma Creek; the Nakai's and Lameman's of Red Mesa; the Atene's and Manheimer's of Navajo Mountain

The community of support includes the Utah Arts Council, David Rockefeller Jr. and the Rockefeller Brothers Fund Award for Excellence in Arts Education Program, Utah State Office of Education, San Juan County School District; and the Red Mesa, Navajo Mountain and Aneth Chapters of the Navajo Tribe. To all of the classroom teachers I have worked with I say thank you for working with me for the good of the children.

My work with children was inspired by many. The following individuals informed my thinking and offered continued support: Susan Beck, Sue Heath, Glenna Sam, Vicki Joe, Bernice Holly, Paul Pitts, Mark E. Peterson, Terry Tempest Williams, Shonto Begay, Steve Darden, Harold and Stella Drake, J. Edson Way, John Schaefer, and my parents; Jeanne and Steve Hucko. Our family also includes Native People's Magazine and the Wheelwright Museum of the American Indian in Santa Fe, New Mexico, the two institutions who first exhibited "Have You Ever Seen a Rainbow at Night?"

Editor Victoria Rock provided valuable insight, thoughtfully guiding the text to its final form. The creative team of Terry Duffy, Ron Schultz, and David Skolkin at Learning Arts Publications saw the book's potential and patiently and diligently worked to make it a reality.

On behalf of the children I extend a heartfelt, "aheehe" (Thank you) to all.

Bruce Hucko
Santa Fe, NM
December, 1995